P9-DDV-036

Weekly Reader Children's Book Club presents

The Cool Ride in the Sky

The Cool Ride

Alfred A. Knopf  New York

in the Sky

Told by Diane Wolkstein

Paul Galdone drew the pictures

For
Charly and Lotty Zucker
my friends and protectors
with great love

This story is an adaptation of the tale "Straighten Up and Fly Right." A dialect version of the tale as told by John Blackamore to Richard Dorson appears in *Western Folklore*, 1955.

The song "Straighten Up and Fly Right," recorded by Nat King Cole, is Copyright 1944 by American Academy of Music, Inc. and used with permission.

I wish to thank Mrs. Nat King Cole for her kind assistance.

THIS IS A BORZOI BOOK PUBLISHED BY ALFRED A. KNOPF, INC.

This title was originally catalogued by the Library of Congress as follows:

Wolkstein, Diane.
The cool ride in the sky. Paul Galdone drew the pictures. New York, Knopf; [distributed by Random House, 1973]

[32] p. col. illus. 29 cm. $4.50

SUMMARY: The monkey gets even with the buzzard for deceiving and devouring two of his friends.

[1. Folklore, Negro. 2. Folklore—United States] I. Galdone, Paul, illus. II. Title.

PZ8.1.W84Co 398.2'452'0973 72-5269
ISBN 0-394-82489-X ISBN 0-394-92489-4 (lib. bdg.)

Manufactured in the United States of America.

Weekly Reader Children's Book Club Edition

The Cool Ride in the Sky

It was a very hot summer day.

All the animals were hiding from the sun under bushes or in their holes, but not the buzzard. He was sailing around in the sky looking for food.

He'd been sailing around for hours, when suddenly—

A rabbit hopped out of his hole. The buzzard quickly spotted him and swooped down, but the rabbit hopped back in his hole.

The buzzard landed beside the rabbit's hole.

"Hello rabbit," said the buzzard sweetly. "How is it down in your hole?"

"Hot!" cried the rabbit. "It's hot in my house and it's hot on the ground. How is it up in the sky?"

"Oh rabbit," said the buzzard. "It's as cool as can be. Why don't you jump on my back and I'll take you up there?"

The rabbit peeked out of his hole. The sun was blazing hot.

"Hurry rabbit," said the buzzard. "I don't have time to be giving free rides to everyone."

The rabbit looked at the buzzard. The buzzard looked so cool and pleased that the rabbit decided to take a chance. "Okay," he said, and hopped onto the buzzard's back.

The buzzard flew up in the sky. He sailed around and around, until he was ready for lunch. "Hold on rabbit," he said. "I'm going down for a landing."

Then the buzzard went into his power dive, a hundred feet straight down. Just before he hit the earth, he shot up again throwing the rabbit from his back. The buzzard then turned in the air, flew back to the ground and ate the rabbit for lunch.

Late that afternoon the buzzard was hungry again. He flew to the same place and circled around in the sky, around and around, until—

A squirrel scampered down from his nest. Quickly the buzzard headed for the squirrel, but the squirrel dashed back into a hole in the tree.

The buzzard landed on one of the branches.

"Hello squirrel!" the buzzard called. "How are you feeling today?"

"I'm hot, buzzard. It's been hot all day and I'm still hot."

"It's cool in the sky, squirrel. Jump on my back and I'll take you up there."

Now the squirrel *knew* the buzzard was a tricky animal, but he also knew that the higher in a tree you go, the cooler it is, still—

"Jump on my back," said the buzzard, "or maybe you're afraid to fly so high?"

"Of course not!" said the squirrel. He jumped onto the buzzard's back and up they flew.

Meanwhile, a monkey who was sitting in the branches of a nearby tree had been watching the buzzard. He'd seen the trick the buzzard had played on the rabbit, and now he was watching to see what the buzzard would do with the squirrel.

The buzzard sailed around and around.

After a while the buzzard turned to the squirrel and said: "Hold on, squirrel. I'm going down for a landing."

Again the buzzard went into his power dive, a hundred feet straight down, shooting up again at the last minute, throwing the poor squirrel off his back. Then the buzzard turned, flew back and ate the squirrel for dinner.

After the buzzard had flown off, the monkey began to swing on his branch. Back and forth, back and forth until—he got an idea.

The next day it was hot again. The sun was shining brightly, and the animals were hiding from the sun. But the monkey was standing in plain sight watching the sky.

When the other animals saw the monkey standing hour after hour in the hot sun, they became more and more curious and poked their heads further out of their hiding places.

Towards noon, the monkey spotted the buzzard. He began to dance up and down, flapping his arms in the air. In less than a minute the buzzard was down on the ground beside the monkey.

"Hello monkey," he said. "What kind of dance were you doing?"

"A flying dance. Did you like it?"
"Well . . . yes—"
"Yes," said the monkey. "I was doing a flying dance, just *wishing* I could go for a cool ride in the sky."
"Oh-h monkey!" The buzzard's face broke into a great big grin. "There's nothing I like more than giving free rides in the sky. Quick, jump on my back and up we go."

The monkey winked at the other animals and slowly seated himself on the buzzard's back.

The buzzard took off. He circled around once in the sky. Then he turned to the monkey and said: "Hold on monkey, I'm going down for a landing."

"HOLD ON!" the monkey shouted back.
"THERE'S GOING TO BE NO MONKEY DINNER TONIGHT!"

And the monkey whipped his tail out and wrapped it so tight around the buzzard's neck that the buzzard's eyes nearly popped out of his head.

"BUZZARD!" said the monkey, "YOU STRAIGHTEN UP AND FLY RIGHT!"

The buzzard was caught and had to fly straight on.

The monkey ordered the buzzard to fly low, so he could wave to his friends on the ground. They cheered and waved back.

"Now then buzzard," said the monkey, "up we go." And the buzzard flew up again in the cool air and sailed around in the sky, until—

The *monkey* was ready to go down. The monkey loosened his hold ever so slightly on the buzzard's neck, and the buzzard glided down to a soft landing.

All the animals crowded around the monkey laughing and cheering, while the buzzard flew off in shame.

"We won't be seeing that buzzard again for a long time," said the monkey.

Then he flapped his arms in the air and began to hop from foot to foot. He was doing the flying dance.

And soon all the animals joined him.

Nat King Cole first heard the story of the buzzard and the monkey from his father, a Baptist minister in Montgomery, Alabama. He then recorded "Straighten Up and Fly Right," based on the story, in 1943. Here is a part of that song.